LA Sykes
Mancheste[r]
and criminology before working for a decade in acute psychiatry and spent two years working at Wigan and Leigh Disability Partnership.

His work has been up at the likes of Shotgun Honey, Lurid Lit, Nightmare Illustrated, Blink Ink and others and has appeared in the Dog Horn Press *punkPunk!* anthology with a story co-written with Mark Slade.

His work has been podcasted at Blackout City and Dark Dreams.

He can be contacted at **sykesfiction@live.co.uk**.

Photo by: Darryl Kinney

"Every step leaves ex DI Ben Pitkin wrestling with his own sanity, takes him deeper into seedy shadows thick with money and greed, deeper into the sickness of a country tearing itself apart under the pressures of austerity. Northern Noir at its most fierce, Sykes' novella takes a hard, cold look at the desperate actions of desperate people caught in the effects of psychological trauma." —**E.S. Wynn**

"This is hardboiled noir. This is updated noir. This is a book you have to read." —**Joseph Patchen**, *Lurid Lit*

"A surprisingly dark, thoughtful, action filled, hardboiled thriller with a heart as black as pitch. If you like dark fiction, this is it." —**Christopher Black**

By the same author

Noir Medley

Knuckle Cracking Novellas
12

THE HARD COLD SHOULDER

A Novella

By L.A. Sykes

Close To The Bone
An imprint of Gritfiction Ltd

Copyright © 2017 by L.A. Sykes

First published in Great Britain in 2013 by Thunderune as an Ebook

ISBN 978-1-97339-629-1

All rights reserved. No part of the book may be produced in any form or by any electronic or mechanical means, including information storage and retrieval systems, without permission in writing from the publisher, except by a reviewer who may use brief quotations in a book review.

Close To The Bonee
an imprint of Gritfiction Ltd
Rugby
Warwickshire
CV21
www.close2thebone.co.uk

The characters and events in this book are fictitious. Any similarity to real persons, living or dead, is coincidental and not intended by the author.

Cover and Interior Design by Craig Douglas

First Printing, 2017

The Hard Cold Shoulder

1

I was already knee deep in hopeful guilt cheques from those who cared too late about the probable dead, sat on the North Western train station platform bench next to the payphone at dusk, when the call came from small town loser Tommy Rellis. The same long time gambling addict and brain dead, bottom-rung insurance fraudster I'd nicked on numerous occasions in the decade I'd served as a detective for the Greater Manchester Police before things went awry. The swagger from his once broad shoulders had dissipated and spread to his once cocky voice but I recognised the distinctive nasal whine immediately; static garble scratched at my eardrum, followed by: "Detective Pitkin, is that you?"

"Just Pitkin, Tommy. What can I do you for?"

"I want, no, need her back, Mr. Pitkin. It went too far, way too far. I can't live like this, with this. You need to get her back, before it's too late. I mean, far as me and her goes it probably is too late, I can't see how she'll ever forgive me but, Jesus, I can't leave it like this. Please, I've got money now."

I could smell the pleading despair on his breath through the wires. I never asked any of them how they'd know I was there and never asked for any up front from a client on the wrong side of the edge. I never needed to and never wanted to. Worst case scenario I could end up balls deep in a mess with my prints on half a fee and my old employers with a grip on my shoulder. So I made a habit of staying clean until curtain call with the desperate. Tommy fell face first into that category. Those like Tommy, drowning in their predicaments, never needed preamble small talk either and I liked it that way.

"Who's her?"

"My daughter, Tabitha. My only kid and all, what was I thinking-"

"You'll have to ask a psychologist about that. When was the last time you saw her?"

"God, must be months I think-"

"Months? Crisis of conscience struck you, Tommy?"

"Fuck you. You have to understand, man, the ex has an injunction out on me. I'm not allowed to go within a mile of 'em. I'd tried to just push 'em out of my mind, like, because there's no way I'm doing more jail time and that bitch would have loved to get me locked up again. I…I was going through tough times, you…you have to understand. Then I heard she was up at the Royal at the A and E. There's a nurse I'd been fucking, Sandra, she phoned me up. She recognised the name, said she'd O.D.'d on the Brown and was lucky to live through it. She was only there a couple of hours when he picked her up and took her. She looked in a state and thought I should know, said she should have been kept in longer. It was supposed to be over by now, it didn't go the way we planned. Was supposed to be a straight forward kidnap deal, I thought I'd proper put the wind up the bitch ex, scare her to death like, and get back a chunk of that child support she's probably pissed up the wall, you know, and then maybe I'd pay off my debts and have a shot at custody. But he, he -," the voice cracked and sobs wet my ear.

The Glasgow to London Euston idled into the station; headlights pierced the darkness, the screeching brakes muffled the spatter of rainfall.

"Go on," I prompted, failing to keep the contempt out of my voice.

He cleared his throat and continued, "He said it'd be easy. He said he'd keep her comfortable, safe you know, till the drop off. Soon as we had the money, we'd get her back safe and everything would be hunky dory," grated laughter and weeping, "he fucking backed out. He phoned and said he was tipped off the cops were onto us and we'd be picked up when we showed up for the money and he had no choice but to make money off her in the long run instead. I begged him to just give her back and call it all off as a bad job but he…he just laughed and put the phone down on me. I've been all over Greater Manchester, every fucking back street all hours day and night. I've seen nothing of her. I didn't know where he even lived or where he was going to keep her. I never even asked, and how can I go to the police? How? I'd be strung up, an accomplice to his own daughter's kidnap. You need to help me…" The voice broke in to hysterics.

I took his address down with the promise that

I'd show for payment regardless of result and nothing else.

He sobbed louder as he choked out her description and distinguishing features; the vividness of her in my mind's eye needed no note taking and it would remain there for long, long after.

I gave him a few seconds to compose himself then

asked, "Who's he?"

"The Joey."

"Joey who?"

"No, he's called The Joey. Fuck knows his real name, I never asked. I never even asked, what the fuck was I thinking? Met him at a backroom card game somewhere, a pub off King Street I think, a while back. Got to talking and…and I've tried tracking him down and nobody knows who he is, or even if they do they don't want to tell me. What was I thinking?" His voice broke again.

"I'll come for the money when it's over," I repeated.

"Bring her back safe, Mr. Pitkin, I'm so so sorry, please bring her bac-"

"If I bring her back safe, I'm taking every penny you've got."

"Hang on, every penny? That's a bit harsh-"

I hung up the phone and watched the train gear up for departure. Blank faces stared out at the deserted platform, giving me as long a look as the bench and the swirling litter.

I headed up the concrete steps and past the night ticket master. He regarded me with the same empathic look every night, "Still no show of her, mister?" He asked with a sympathetic smile.

I forced a smile back and shook my head.

He'd forged the idea I was waiting for a long lost love to come back and reunite with me in an empty train station in the North West at dusk on a cold, rain swept night. I never put him straight. In a way, maybe he was right. Maybe I was and I didn't want to realise. In the end I convinced myself of it. I called her Hope and dreamed she had a warm embrace and sweet perfume and two one way tickets to far, far away

I waved him goodnight and stood in the acidic downpour for a while in this year of Our Lord two thousand and thirteen, letting it melt away fleeting flights of fancy until reality stepped in with the hard cold shoulder.

2

I jumped a black cab to the Royal Infirmary, ignoring the driver's rote comments about flood warnings and thunderstorms brewing in the thick blanket of clouds smothering the moonlight. I told him to wind down all the windows.

"It's Baltic, man," he replied in a thick Scottish brogue.

"Open them all, now," I shouted, my body tensing. I could have sworn I heard him mutter *nutcase* under his breath. "What did you say?"

"You're the boss, I said."

The air took the edge off and I pushed my arm out of the window, concentrating on the stinging in my hand from the harsh elements.

Rounding the corner at the top of the sloped street, lines of protesters had set up stall for the night, campaigning against the Conservative – Lib Dem public service slashes. Fierce chants mingled with jovial solidarity in the lashing rain, placards hoisted roadside. Traffic crawled slowly with drivers beeping and shouting words of encouragement. I caught sight of signs in bold red lettering, one saying:

SAVING THE NHS IS SAVING OUR SELVES,

another:

CONNING AND DEMOLISHING – FAILED AT MAJORITY ELECTION, FAILED ON PROMISES.

My stomach twisted; the sentiments displayed reminded me of the outraged militancy running through the station when the austerity cuts hit the police force. Speeches in the canteen and standing shoulder to shoulder in camaraderie for right and just and safe streets and our presence and I pined for the bland food and the stale coffee and the damp office and shambolic chaos of live incident rooms crackling with nervous excitement. I forced the rose tinting nostalgia away remembering the hypocrisy, recalling protest containment war stories told by some older coppers, laughing as they described waving money at starving miners and taking their numbers off their shoulders as they described wading into picket lines on horseback. I saw their fond memories dance in their eyes, lighting up their faces, memories of being drafted in on overtime for battles with people giving the big *no* to the policy makers in the Poll Tax Riots back in '90. I realised I was better off neutral to the whole game.

The driver seemed to read my thoughts.

Pulling into the car park he said, "Takes you back, don't it laddie? Thatcher and that fucking poll tax. What a kerfuffle that was. These tossers in now, they idolise the old bitch. They'd better enjoy their time in power, I'm telling you, 'cos they won't be getting back in for decades after the mess they're making. They're too far removed from the common struggle, them without the head starts in life, like. Fuck's sake, I read in the paper the other day a cripple topped hisself 'cos he'd been told his disability money was being cut. A cripple, man, can you believe that? And they're saying they're going to spend millions on Thatcher's funeral. Beggars fucking belief."

"It'll be for security, mostly, I'd imagine."

"What kind of corpse needs millions of pounds for security purposes? Fuck's sake. And these tossers idolise her? Can't support your living disabled but they can spend millions protecting a corpse and her funeral from being wrecked? Beggars fucking belief."

I shrugged. "I'm not really into politics."

He snatched the tenner from my outstretched arm. Charles Darwin's ghostly face beamed luminous in what looked like consternation on the note in the overhead light. "Politics? It's about humanity, not fucking policy, man. This country is heading for disaster," he screeched through the window. I left him to it and dawdled for a minute in the open space.

***

The hospital's red brick Victorian parapets jutted into the sable sky. Its ambulance bay was empty of vehicles and scattered with dressing gowned smokers on drips, shivering under the modern addition of a slanting fibreglass porch shelter. A queue weaved through the main entrance doors from the A and E department desk and I forced myself forward, shoved my way in between makeshift bloodied bandages and relentless retching into the adjacent medical admissions unit.

A gaggle of night nurses sat gossiping around the front desk about the industrial action. I picked out the senior staff and pulled her aside by flashing my GMP emblem with my ring finger over the validity date and my middle finger over the name, keeping the mug shot visible.

She smoothed out her uniform, the smile faded from her rouge lips and a crease forged itself in the centre of her forehead.

Another nurse giggled and said, "Watch out for his truncheon Vanessa, especially if his handcuffs are furry."

Vanessa flushed and replied, "Haven't you got work to be getting on with?" failing to pull off an authoritative tone.

I waved my warrant card around and addressed the giggling staff. "This floor could do with mopping. And haven't you got patients to attend to? Or are you on strike in here, hiding from the cold?" They shared a snigger and busied themselves shuffling papers.

"Vanessa, where can we get some privacy? I won't keep you long."

She gestured to an empty office down the corridor. I took a deep breath to steady myself for the cramped alcove and went in, she following me without hesitation. Before her backside touched the chair I said, "Tabitha Rellis was admitted here last night with a heroin overdose. What did she say, who'd she leave with, and when?" The nurses' hand tremored and dilating blue irises darted around.

"I, Officer —"

"Detective"

"Detective, you know I can't give out that kind of information without good reason."

"I've got a good reason, Vanessa love. I'm guessing by your shakes you were on duty when you discharged her. I'm guessing the bloke you discharged her into the care of didn't look so legit on reflection. I'm guessing you're shitting bricks round about now because you failed to trigger child protection given she's fifteen. I'm guessing she never even spoke to you, nor you her. I'm guessing you took all the information from the bloke and had a slight distrust that she was twenty from the fake D.O.B. he gave but you were either too intimidated or too busy to check. I'm guessing you wrote her off as a junkie anyway. I'm guessing you went home that morning and it scratched around in the back of your mind for a while, the girls face, looking peaceful. Too peaceful for a fifteen year old in the company of a stranger and who's got oblivion ripping through her bloodstream. But they're gone now, and there's a thousand more winging their way here in the back of a box with blue lights. I'm guessing you eventually slept and slept well and when you woke up she was nothing more than a faded nightmare. I'm guessing we have a good reason to talk."

She struggled to sip water from a small plastic cup through increasing shakes and hunched over fiddling with a blister pack of Diazepam. I reached down and popped a yellow into her palm, slipping the rest of the foil packet into my black overcoat. She gulped and stared at the lime green wall and started to talk with a waver in her whispering voice.

"I had my suspicions she wasn't twenty. I mean, she was thin and had such a small frame on her, but, who isn't on heroin? He, well, he looked mad, *angry mad*, when he carried her into the emergency department. I saw them coming in, I was having a fag at the entrance. She was out of it, her head bobbing, she looked…well, she looked dead to be honest. They'd brought her straight through to us by the time I'd got back in. We dripped her up, nothing fancy, and let the drugs wear off. Poor bugger was worn out, all she managed to say in the time she was with us was her name, just the once and all. We told him to leave her till at least the morning, but he insisted on taking care of her. He looked angry like I said. You know, comes home, finds his daughter off her head on drugs, you can understand it, us letting them go can't you, especially being twenty, twenty is a grown adult. We can't jus-"

"What was the address he gave?"

She rifled through a metal filing cabinet, pulled out a red cardboard file and mumbled a street of terraced state houses that had been condemned by the council eight months ago. The street was bulldozed rubble now.

"Where'd the ambulance pick her up?"

"It didn't. He brought her. It was a Silver Tigra, I remember that. I remember seeing the doors left wide open. He left it in the ambulance bay when he carried her in. I remember when security came to have him shift it. Come to think of it, apart from then he never left her side all the time they were here."

"Registration?" She shrugged her shoulders, then pushed back from me as I swore under my breath.

"What did he look like?"

"Mr Rellis? Thin, dark eyes, five foot five or thereabouts." Half a foot smaller than the Tommy Rellis I knew.

"Anything else you remember that I should know about?"

She shook her head and made eye contact for the first time, "I, well, I want to ask about discretion, I mean…not for my sake, but the reputation of the Trust. The government wants to shut us down, make everything private, a scandal or something would give them plenty of ammunition, if you know what I mean. They're trying to make out it's our fault that there are no beds and ridiculous waiting times. As though we're incompetent or lazy, instead of telling the truth that they've left us with too little staff to run the place. God, they'd love a story like this, with the strike and all. Especially the strike, can you imagine the headlines? It had nothing to do with that, detective, I can assure you. We were staffed as normal, covered, which isn't saying much I know, but you know what I mean. We weren't short because of it, is what I'm trying to say. I should have said or done something, Jesus, I could get struck off for this."

I stared hard at her shaking head and twitching

hand rippling the surface of the water in the cup. "I've no control over that. I'm sure you all do your best, but just remember for the future that nobody is *just a junkie*. Because we all are, for some things, aren't we?" I said, nodding at the discarded benzodiazepine box. "One more thing before I leave you to get back to work. What can you tell me about Sandra, your A and E colleague?"

She frowned distractedly and said, "Sorry? What?"

"Sandra, from A and E. What can you tell me?"

"Red haired Sandra? She's off sick with stress. That's what they say she's off with. Stress, eh? I don't think I've met anyone working here without stress, with all what's going on and this bloody bureaucracy on top, like there's not enough to do. You'd know, being the police. They're doing the same to you lot aren't they? Why, she's alright isn't she, I mean you don't thi-"

"Doesn't matter, just wanted a quick word, but the bloody bureaucrats on her ward wouldn't give me her address."

She shook her head and laughed incredulously, "Really? That's ridiculous. I know she's in the nurses accommodation block, I just don't know the number. Sorry I can't be more helpful, and I'm sorry about the…the other thing."

I nodded, "I'll get it off the computer at the station, no bother. I'll leave you to get back to your patients."

I walked out down the corridor through the bleeding and bouncing A and E rabble with her words running after my eardrums: "Please let me know Theresa's all right."

"Tabitha," I shouted.

***

Children screaming and parents tutting from the A and E queue snatched my attention. The line had splayed into a circle. In the middle, two security guards wrestled with a drunk. They were unevenly matched, one being over six foot, the other just about five. The figure in between took advantage of the mismatch, leaning into the shorter.

I walked over to see if I'd know the bloke, thinking it was probably one of the known street drunks left to rot and beg in the high street, thinking I could talk him down before someone got hurt. I was surprised by the drunk's sharp suit as he shouted, "Get off me you grubby bastards and give me my glasses."

I waved my I.D. at the security boys. The taller grimaced, keeping a tight grip on the suit's wrist and said, "Your lot's back, eh? Should think so too, should be in't cells, this bugger. Your lot brought him in, pissed out of his face dancing around in town. They couldn't be arsed with arresting him, told the staff to let him go when he's sober and passed fit. Was alright at first, slept like. Since he's woke up he's demanding to jump the queue. We weren't funny with him, we just told him no, and then he goes to slap Danny," nodding to the smaller guard.

He managed a smile while struggling to restrain the other sinewy arm and chipped in, "He did and all, good job I can still bob and weave."

Taller strained and growled, "Keep still, calm down. Danny, get that wrist lock on proper, don't bruise his skin, Christsakes, we'll be sued, sacked or both."

The drunk wriggled and turned to the taller guard, "How dare you-"

I cut his speech off by slapping him across the face with the warrant card. "No, how dare you. How dare you act like this in front of kids. This is a bloody hospital. For everybody, not just you. You're no more important than anybody else, so either sit down, shut up and wait your turn, or fuck off home. These people work here to help people, you jumped up prick. Treat them with proper respect or sling it."

He stopped struggling, breathing heavily.

"The cavalry, I see. You're just a glorified version of these clowns. Do yourself a favour and piss off."

I laughed and took the wrist from the taller guard. I twisted it hard and shoved it up his back, kicking away his legs. Pushed his face into the floor, knelt down and whispered, "Buck up, buttercup. You're making a prize fool of yourself."

"Get off! You can't do this. I'll report you, you vicious little thug. You're going to break my arm."

"Are you going to behave?"

"Don't dare talk to me like a child, you-," I pressed his wrist higher. He yelped.

"Well, stop acting like one. Now are we finished?"

"You're finished! you're finished, you hear me?"

"I'm not finished just yet." I ground my knuckle into his nose. He squealed.

"Just get off."

"Only when I'm satisfied you're going to be civilized." He wisely kept his mouth shut and I let go. I dragged him back to his feet, picked up his glasses and delicately slid them onto his shocked face.

I turned to leave, pushing through the clapping crowd.

"Never even said thank you for returning his glasses, the rude bugger," I said to a young woman with two dumbstruck kids clamped to her thighs on my way out.

I followed the signs to the nurses' residency block, wondering what had happened to the country to take it to the point where nurses were on yellow pills and going against their vocation to stage a strike because of the decisions of politicians who couldn't get a majority vote and considered human suffering in economic terms, forgetting about the people with nothing but the rain as a surety.

I'd been harsh on the nurse, Vanessa, maybe too harsh. I didn't think I'd been too harsh on the Champagne Charlie and I convinced myself I'd broken even on the karma front.

The front entrance to the nursing residential block, a squat, grey-bricked huddle of flats, was locked with an electronic keypad, making a discrete break-in impossible. I tried a couple of random codes hoping to get lucky. I pushed all the buzzers, numbered one to forty, and got nothing in the way of a response.

Karma shone in the form of a pretty brunette who gave me a smile that could sweep the streets. She unclipped the door and said, "Can I help you?"

I tried a smile and said, "I'm a friend of Sandra's, love. You know, bright red hair. Just passing by and wanted a quick catch up, like."

"Sandra? Oh I know, yes, she's on the top floor at the end. That Sandra?"

"That's the one. Thirty-eight."

"Thirty-six, isn't it? I might be wrong, I've only been there once, for a coffee when I first moved here. I've not see her in ages, come to think of it. Shift work. Tell her hello from Emma on the ground floor, will you?"

"Certainly, Emma. Off anywhere nice?"

"Just into town meeting some friends."

"Well, have a good one. And take care, now."

"Thanks." She let herself out and I watched her disappear at the end of the street. I took the stairs; the landings were silent, most of the flats seemed unoccupied with only the odd one on each floor with mats and shoe trays outside their doors. I reached the top floor. Eight doors, four either side. Thirty-six, second on the right.

I crept across the moss green carpet, listened hard. Nothing. I tapped lightly on the door. No response. I slowly depressed the handle. It was locked. I listened again, took another look around and remembered I wasn't a copper any more anyway. What was I afraid of? I didn't need just cause and magistrates permission to jeopardise legal process.

No more disciplinary board meetings.

No bollockings.

Fuck it.

I stepped back and took it off its hinges with my shoulder, swinging into the flat's wall with a sharp crack.

The living room doubled as a bedroom with a small kitchen attached at the top; its door open. It was empty. The bed wasn't. Its occupant remained static. Either a deep sleeper or worse. I took a deep breath to steady myself from the room shrinking in my mind; I felt the walls pressing against my shoulders.

I rushed to the still form, head concealed under a thick white duvet. I gripped the covers and prepared for the worst. I peeled them back and piercing screams threw me back in a panicked scramble.

A naked Indian man sat bolt upright, letting out shrieks in staccato bursts.

"Shush, whoa, calm down. Calm down," I shouted.

He jumped out of bed and reached underneath, pulling out a cricket bat. "Come on, pervert. I'll take your fucking kneecaps off!" he cried, wild eyed.

I snatched my warrant card, waving it. "It's alright, I'm the police. There's nothing to be alarmed about-"

"Nothing to be alarmed about!? I've been on call for the last twenty-four hours and the minute I get to sleep the police come kicking my door in! I've been a tax paying British citizen for twenty-eight years and I get treated like this? Do you want proof you fascist bastard? I'll get you proof." He dropped the bat and started rifling through a drawer under a bedside table.

I shouted to his back, "No, no, no there's no need for any of that. I just got the addresses mixed up, that's all. Just a welfare check on someone doctor, that's all."

"Doctor? I'm a Mister, you rude bastard. Consultant. Can you even spell that? I bet you can't even say it, you uncultured yob. Go on, say it."

"Look, Mister, I've got my job to do so I'm going to have to leave now. I apologize for the disturbance, now go back to sleep."

"Say it."

"What?"

"Consultant. As in consult, to ask. Ask, instead of knocking bloody doors off hinges when people are trying to sleep. You can't even say it, can you? Too many syllables hasn't it?"

My patience thinned quickly. "Oh fuck off back to bed."

"Oh I will, Mr. big policeman, kicking in doors. I'll go back to sleep when I've phoned security."

I left him jabbering to himself and fiddling with his phone. I went back into the corridor and saw thirty-eight had the only other floor mat. Dried mud crusted around its edges. I had maybe two minutes before the security boys would show.

Shouldered into thirty-eight; identical layout except for an untouched bed. The kitchen was as bare as the walls. Under the bed, two black canvas bags with clothes packed tightly, ceramic ornaments wrapped with socks. A half-full strip of syringes in a side pocket with toiletries. Nurse Sandra, possible junkie or major league diabetic. Packed and ready to bolt.

I came out of the room, wedging the door shut behind me and hoping the dim lights would cover the splintered edges. Shouted from the doorway of thirty-six, "Sir, when was the last time you saw your neighbour?"

"I'm so tired I don't know what fucking day it is. The security are coming for you," he smiled under his bushy moustache.

"Think. She may be at risk. I was told she's off sick with stress, I need to know when you last saw her."

"Stress? Ha! She'd know what stress is if she had to put up with this kind of harassment! I can't remember the exact day, a week or so ago, maybe." He swung his arms up in the air, "She's probably ran away, and I can't blame her. Who in their right mind would want to live in this town!?'

I left him to it and bolted down the stairs. I approached the front door and saw the security boys letting themselves in with a key fob. I had nowhere to hide and contemplated on which one to knock out first. The taller broke into a smile and said, "Oh, it's you, inspector. We couldn't recognise you through the glass. We thought you were a burglar or something."

I forced a laugh. "No, was just passing through and heard a commotion. I'm glad you two are here. Some naked Indian bloke was running about with a cricket bat. Think he was sleepwalking, talking about having a nightmare about being deported. I managed to wake him up and took him back to his flat. He's made a mess of a couple of doors though. Must have been a vivid dream, I'll say that."

Danny and the taller man turned to each other and said, "Mr Kadam," simultaneously.

"Got to shoot lads. Tuck him in properly."

"We will, thanks for before."

"Any time, boys."

The rain outside carried on the rising wind, lashing my face. I was dizzy: from the cramped spaces and the fact the nurse, Sandra, couldn't have been on duty the night Tabitha was admitted. Yet she knew enough to inform Tommy Rellis of the details. I wondered how that was possible and my head thumped at the implications and the image of packed bags; ready to disappear. Waves of exhaustion swayed my balance and I welcomed the icy bite of the gale to keep me alert. Things didn't add up and I needed a rest and some back up, in the form of thirteen bullets.

3

I walked down the canal bank and up over the iron bridge to my flat, trying to burn off the adrenalin the agoraphobic panic had shot into my veins, hoping the serenity of the slow flowing grey canal water would rub off on me; neither the walk nor water made any difference.

Crossing the deserted road I heard light tapping a distance behind. They sounded more and more like footsteps the longer and harder I listened.

I kept walking at the same pace for a hundred metres, stopping suddenly and crouching, playing with my boot laces. The footsteps followed suit. Only the humming of the orange lamp post bulb broke the silence. I chanced a look around, seeing nothing and anything in a menagerie of sinister black forms, sculpting random patterns from neon lit shadows.

The effects of insomnia were worsening by the day, teasing my senses, and I scanned the street until I was sure there was nothing.

I took the stairs to the third floor of the block I never called home. Kicked my way through a pile of post and flipped on the light. Buzzing television sets from the thin walls of the neighbours scratched at the silence I craved.

The hallway seemed narrower every time I came back, even though I felt myself growing smaller. I went into the living room, leaving the doors wide open, and slid the windows up, welcoming the wind. I ran a freezing shower and tried to slow down my thoughts and the choking sensation of the cramped bathroom.

I knew Tommy Rellis was owed no pity, but I felt the torture of the man's bad decision-making creeping into my fibres; echoes of my own mistakes illuminated in the bare, one bedroom flat with Closed In for unwanted constant company. The consequences of the man's disgusting, selfish stupidity spiked into the forefront of my mind, ripping up ruminations of both mine and Tommy's self-induced annihilation: The girl, Tabitha.

Her name flickered round and round and visions of streams of tears swam through my head and I forced myself to lie on my bed and clamp shut my eyes. Beads of sweat cascaded from my temples and I concentrated on breathing steadily, willing desperately needed sleep to carry me away.

Flashes of fragmented faces danced and I focused on fading them to black through the shattered lenses of my eyes taking refuge and writhing behind the lids fighting to open. My body locked up and I drifted into the moment where consciousness unravels onto the sweet edge of the realm of the promise of sleep. I floated towards a flush meadow and saw a scattering of red carnations swaying gently. I swept my hand down to feel the petals and the flowers wilted between my fingertips. The white clouds gathered together, darkening and twisting the sky as shadows towered and a ripping gust stole my breath. Thunderous rain peppered the earth, soddening the ground until I felt it fall away. I scrambled back up on a mound of mud, dirt sinking beneath my feet. The ground rumbled and shook and I turned to see a great caliginous hole with limbs clawing at the surface. Copious legions of corpses broke through, various shapes and sizes, naked flesh peeling from their emaciated bodies and faces, pulling each other up, following my path, begging me with their eyes, circling and snatching at my feet and murmuring and squealing. I tried to scramble higher but their bloodied arms reached out and yanked at my legs. Swirling clouds descended and wrapped around my chest and neck, dragging me skyward though the dead hung on, splaying my body, separating the vertebrae in my stretched back.

I was screaming, my screams uncontrollable, screwing into my skull and ringing my ears and I forced my eyelids to open and gasped for breath. I ran into the living room, leaned out of the window, shivering, sucking in air. I felt a presence emanating from the hall and snapped my head around.

DCI Tavistock raised his eyebrows and grinned from the doorway.

4

He shook his head slowly, sighed and said, "What's up with your face? You look like you've been in't woods wit Yorkshire Ripper."

He was my gaffer, before the force psychologists told me I wasn't mentally strong enough anymore. They told me what I was experiencing was perfectly normal. They told me one day I'd be more or less back to my old self. Maybe. I told them I could function fine for the job.

More than fine. Good to go, keen to get back in the station, elbow to elbow with the crew. The Brass wouldn't take my word for it, and wouldn't have let Tavistock's thoughts on the matter shift their decision anyway.

I tried to compose myself and shrugged. "How are you doing, sir?"

"Been better, lad, been better, but looking at you puts things into perspective a bit, that's for certain. Just thought I'd pop in, keep tabs like." He looked around the living room, scrunched up his face at the veil of dust layering the glass coffee table and the brown faux leather couch, "Hardly the Casino here, lad, is it? Don't you offer guests a drink?"

"I don't have any, sir. I don't drink, I like to keep my mind sharp," I said, forcing a smile.

He stared into my eyes, "How times change, eh? No booze? What is it? Scared you'll lose control and do something stupid?"

I took a deep breath and felt my face burn. I kept the forced smile fixed. "No, my mind is fine alright. I just prefer to keep it clear is all."

He looked me up and down. "That right, is it? You used to drown yourself in ale. You been eating? I've seen more meat on a butcher's pencil."

"Have you come to do a fucking welfare check or what?" I snapped.

He smirked and held up his hands. "All right, all right. You never used to have a temper on you, you touchy bugger. Laid back Larry they used t'say behind your back. I just wanted to show you that you aren't on your own, son. So what are you up to then?"

"Working. Private consultations."

"Consultations, eh? Very posh."

"Best thing that's ever happened. The force's loss. If they won't employ me, there's others who will. No paperwork either, suits me fine. Sit down, sir."

He continued to stare and said, "Prefer to stand, lad. Is that Ludo?" he asked, pointing to the bookcase. "Jesus, I've not played that since I was a nipper. Set it up, I'll have you a game."

"What, now?"

"Should I come back on shrove Tuesday? Course, now. Set it up. Let me wallow in memory lane."

I took down the game, my fingers making indents in the grime on the box. I placed the coloured pieces on the starting circles. "What colour do you want to be, sir?"

"I'll take blue and yellow. You take red and green, I'm sure you know the old saying," he smirked, "you roll first."

I dinked the die, a four.

"Your turn, sir."

He shook his head. "You roll for me."

"You scared to get your prints on it? You don't need to worry, it's legit. I'm not hard up enough be nicking board games just yet."

"Aye, roll for me."

I rolled for Tavistock, a six straight away.

He winked. "Take out the blue."

I rolled again, another six.

"Take out the yellow."

I ground my teeth. Rolled again.

A gust of wind billowed the curtains, flapping against the pane.

A third six.

I looked up at him and he cut me off before I could speak. "Don't even bother with your superstitious bollocks sunshine. The number of the Beast, eh? Bollocks. Go back far enough in the scriptures and the number was six one six Believing in superstition is as dangerous as believing in bad luck. It lets the imagination create all kinds. Belief, a powerful thing and not always wise, good or true. Anyway, who says the six is the right way up? Flip em up and what do you get? Three nines." He laughed. "Move the yellow," motioned for me to roll again.

A three. "Shift the yellow again."

I counted out the squares. Eighteen minus three. fifteen. Tabitha's age.

My hand shook; my roll, a six. "Welcome to the game," he said. I brought out the green pawn.

Rolled a two, tapped out the move.

His roll, a two.

"So you're keeping busy, that's the best way, Lad. Either that or get resting up. Move the yellow. What's got your attention at the moment?"

I rolled myself a six, took out a second green. Then a five, moving the first one. I replied, "Remember Tommy Rellis?"

"Vaguely."

"Used to forge signatures on benefit books and that kind of stuff, the odd batch of stolen goods. Proper talks through his nose."

"Rings a bell. Go on."

"He's hired me to find his daughter. Apparently he and a bloke called The Joey set up a fake kidnap to bleed money out of his ex wife, only his partner's backed out and is keeping the girl as an earner in other ways."

"So you're working for scum now are you lad?"

"I'm employed directly by the people. Cutting out the middlemen, gaffer. Can't see the difference, I was working for the people before anyway, before they made me quit-"

"They didn't make you, you resigned of your own will. Don't think I don't know-"

"It was either that or an office job somewhere in the basement, Tavistock. Don't you fucking judge me. You know full well I'm better out and about." I sent the die skittering off the table onto the floor and sat forward, fists tensing.

He ignored my posturing and bent down.

"It's a six. Move the blue piece." I thumped the six squares, making the other pieces jump, "now pick up the dice-"

"Die"

"Sorry?"

"Die. Singular. One die, is a die. More than one are dice, sir."

"Does the distinction matter, Pitkin?"

"Does the distinction matter if I work on my own or as part of a department, sir?"

"Strange analogy, that is, lad. I think you need some sleep."

"Fuck off," I shouted. I reached down, snatched the die and rolled.

Another fucking six for Tavistock.

"Move the blue. It's a dodgy predicament for a police officer, even an ex police officer, to start taking money off known criminals, sunshine. Are you sure you're all right, mental wise?"

"I'm not doing anything wrong. I'm not doing it for Tommy, either. It's not his daughter's fault her dad used her. I'll take his money and get her back. Just you watch." I slammed down the die.

A one.

I looked up at Tavistock. He grinned. "Move the blue."

I moved it to the square occupied by my green, replacing it and moving it back to its starting circle.

He said, "Six and six and one is thirteen. Who said thirteen was unlucky, eh? I told you, superstitious bollocks. And it was you who rolled them and all."

I upturned the coffee table, shattering the surface, sending the board skidding into the wall. I stared at the shards. "Always fucking hated that game."

Tavistock chuckled. "Not a bad thing you don't like losing, son. But when you're not willing to play for fear of losing, you're missing out. Missing out, lad. Where's the woman's touch in the place? I can barely remember you with a bloody woman apart from the odd mention you'd chip at us."

"There have been women as a matter of record, sir. Quite a few in fact. And when there were I kept them well away from that bastard job and everything and everybody that went with it. In fact, I'll tell you if you want. If you really want to know why there's no woman's touch in this depressing little waking coffin of an abode, listen closely. Not long before Christmas, me and a girl I was very serious about, we found out we were pregnant. We did up the box room, neutral colour like, it was too early to tell the gender. Anyway, I proposed over a Chinese takeaway the next night. She accepted. A few weeks later I get a call while I'm out doing a visit. Not good news. The baby is dead, miscarried. We hadn't even settled on a name. She was devastated. I keep saying she, she was called Andrea, Andrea Folith. She, Andrea, Andrea was told it had done damage inside, that she'd not be able to carry to term ever again. I came home a couple of days before Christmas and she'd gone. Not even a note. Her dad sent me a letter not long after, inviting me to her funeral. She'd fucking topped herself. Fucking topped herself, man."

I don't know why this was coming out now. It was something I'd thought buried deep inside. It was always there, rippling at the surface, but I'd held it and the thin veneer had eroded. I looked over at Tavistock.

He shook his head, the smile gone. "And you never told any of us. Not nobody sunshine?"

"What for? What would I tell anyone that for? There's nothing could have been said or done to change matters."

"Fuck's sake, we'd have been there for you. Nowt wrong with fucking getting upset, doesn't make you less of a man, you idiot. I think that I can see your problem, you're scared. Scared of losing what you love. That fear is normal, especially with what you've been through, but if you let it overrun you, you'll never get to have another experience or take another chance at happiness. That's an empty existence, Pitkin. You can't always control everything and everybody, look now, even in a silly game. I let you roll the die with your own hand and what happened? You've got to be able to take the losses along with the wins."

"How about you either take your own advice or keep it to your fucking self!" I shouted.

His words had needled me, but I regretted the outburst immediately.

He stared out of the window, itching at his stubbled chin.

I turned away, unable to face him.

"I think you need my advice, sunshine, when you're running blind after somebody without back up or a valid badge. Why don't you call it in anyway? Let them down the station find her? Saving one doesn't bring the lost back. Doesn't work that way, trust me."

"I'm earning a living. The way I want. End of story. End of fucking story. I'm not calling it in either. This is my cop. My fucking cop."

"All right, all right. I'll leave you to it. Don't want to outstay my welcome. Watch yourself, lad. And if you're going to take that pistol, and I advise that you do by the way, make sure you ditch it afterward."

"How did you know about the gun?"

"I just do. It's down as missing. It had already been inventoried before you thought you were slick, swiping it."

"Do you know what? I don't think I give a fuck any more, sir."

I heard him sigh and his voice faded down the hall. He shouted, "It's your life, I suppose. Live it how you will. Finish at the top and work your way down, eh? Take care, now."

I felt my blood pulsing in my temples and went back into the bathroom, my teeth clenched tightly. I unclipped my straight razor and pushed the tip next to my taut carotid artery. I risked a glance in the mirror. My face was worn, sallow. I grimaced, pressed the blade into my neck and my arm tensed. A crunching of splintered glass jolted me. I held my breath and listened: nothing apart from the flapping curtain now. I dropped the razor in the sink. I looked back at myself in the mirror, into my eyes. My reflection melted into the image of a scared girl. I ripped the mirror off the wall and smashed it against the radiator.

***

I dressed in the first suit I'd ever bought myself for plainclothes work when I'd made detective sergeant almost ten years ago; a navy blue single breast. A black silk tie found my fingers, knotting perfectly overtop a white shirt collar. I went back into the living room and to the shelves. I slid out the draughts board, laid it flat and unclipped the hinge. I took out the Browning pistol from beneath the pieces and tucked into the belt of my lower back.

    I'd taken the gun from a confiscated stockpile of an ex-army vet who'd shot up the town library a couple of years ago, unable to cope after being tortured overseas. If Tavistock was telling the truth, the gun would be traceable. I could have gone and bought one anywhere but I'd owe the seller for discretion and I had enough debts to pay so I let it be. When I took it I told myself the gun would do some good some day. Roll the die and let it lie.

    I shrugged my black overcoat on and switched the light out as I exited through the living room into the hall. The buzzing from the television sets gnawed into my temples and I stomped hard down the stairs and out into the cold dense air.

I couldn't remember the last time Tavistock had talked when he visited, whether it was days or weeks. Most of the time he'd come and just sit, not saying anything. Comfortable silences between old friends. Old friends, close colleagues. He was different than most of the newer breed of corporate careerists. Old fashioned hard with old fashioned sensibilities and I looked up to him. If I was honest with myself, I wanted to be him for a long time. But that was gone now. I took a deep breath and my chest rattled hollow.

I shook the ruminations away, forced myself to think about the girl and sprinted into town.

5

The *Jack's Bar* insignia glowed a scarlet red from its navy awning. British flags flapped in the gale at either end. I heaved open the door and scanned the tap room. A faux crystal chandelier hung in the centre of the ceiling, light bouncing off the orange painted walls. I'd known it as a coppers' pub since I'd been in uniform. I'd spent more time in there than in my flat in the days when I could enjoy a drink and trust my mind to shut off into the temporary haven of a blackout.

    A pack of off-duty plainclothes gathered around mahogany tables in the far corner near the dart boards. I made out the droopy ginger moustache of DC Don Iverson and he noticed my presence. The other men and women followed his gaze and went silent in recognition. He reluctantly got up and walked over as the boys nudged each other and mumbled between themselves. "It'll only take a minute, Don."

    He'd carried his pint over and pulled at his 'tache with his free hand. "Better had, Pitkin. Can't be seen with you, can I? You know the score, mate. I told you before, if you need me, phone my mobile. I gave you the number, use it. But not often," he said impatiently. There was a seriousness in his expression I'd never seen before.

"And I told you I've no interest in carrying a mobile. I'm not having those fuckers following my every move whenever they want, tapping my line and eavesdropping. I just nee-"

"Eavesdropping? You're paranoid, man. And anyway, they don't need to track you. Everyone in the cop shop knows you sit int' train station every night like a fucking tramp. Rail cops passed C.I.D. the tapes. They're all laughing at you, Inspec…Ben."

Being addressed with the old professional rank fired a fleeting nostalgia that crept into my chest, prodding my temper. My voice raised just loud enough and I aimed over his shoulder. "You think I give a fuck what they think? Look at 'em, pissed out of their skulls while the town's fucked. You fucking useless bunch of piss artist bast-"

He dragged me outside before I could complete the reunion speech I'd rehearsed night after night on the desolate platform, said, "Knock it off. What, what? What is it you want?"

I glared hard and he took a step back. "You've a short memory, Don. You owe me, you fucking cunt."

He took a long swig that did nothing for his furrowed brow and growled, "You knew how it'd be. You're out. You damn well knew, they told you but you wouldn't listen. You quit, remember? You did that. I'm still in, remember. I can't do owt for you, you know that. I don't know what you're playing at in front of them lot. I told you, be discrete and I'll do my best for you on the sly whenever I can, but no, not Ben Pitkin, you have to come barging in here, showing me up and showing yourself up. What? What the fuck do you want?"

Deep down I knew he was right but I gave him a left hook anyway.

He dropped the beer glass, shattering on the cobbles, and staggered back.

I grabbed his tie and pulled his head close. "I'm sorry to disappoint you, but I'm not going to apologise for gate crashing your gathering. I don't have the time for good graces. There's a girl missing. What do you know about a kidnap payoff that never materialized?"

The tie was constricting his throat so I loosened my grip. A little.

"Somebody's having you on Ben. That's not come through to us. We've had missing persons, nothing about a kidnap though, honest."

"Nothing? Well, what have you and the geniuses done about the missing cases? Apart from get pissed?"

I retightened my grip. He choked, "Knock it off will you, we're off shift. Who are you after? Give me a name and I'll ask around."

"Off *shift*." I let go and shoved him against the wall. "You shouldn't need to ask around. Should be up here, lad. In your brain if you had one. Who's The Joey?"

He looked away immediately. "Who?" He said, staring at the cobbles.

I dug my fingers into his cheeks and pushed my face into his. "The Joey," I repeated through my clenched jaw, bored into him.

He looked back for a second, then closed his eyes. He hissed, "You're fucking loco. Do you still see Tavistock?"

His face was bloodied and he was either grinning or grimacing. I hit him like it was the former. "You know what, fuck off back to your pals."

I burst his nose and gave him two more jabs, watching him clatter into the wall and slide down to the deck.

The door swung open and a stocky suit with a skewed tie staggered outside. He brushed the dark hair out of his face, looked down at Iverson and said, "What's going on here?"

"Mind your own."

"It is mine sunshine, I'm the Law."

I took deep breaths and let the hand that instinctively reached for the pistol relax. I laughed.

"I'm going anyway. Who wants to fight the Law?"

As I was walking away, Iverson shouted, "He's fucking dead. Been dead for months, Ben! You need fucking treatment. Sort yourself out, mate."

"Mate? Fuck off."

I walked faster, humming *The Clash* over and over. I cut through the silent, serene churchyard via a short alley across from Jack's Bar and came out into the contrasting raucousness of the revelling crowd lining King Street.

6

King Street was the main through-road of the town centre, housing its hub of nightlife. It heaved and teemed. I pushed through the jostling groups of young partygoers huddled outside the bars smoking cigarettes and entered Retro, an eighties themed dive blaring out Gary Numan's *Cars*. A glitter ball threw globs of light sporadically across the dance floor sparsely populated by middle aged swayers.

Roland 'Beak' Fenk polished glasses with a dirty rag behind the bar. Small time coke shifter and a big nose gave him his nickname. He was my long time GMP informer and I hoped he could earn himself my money.

He greeted me by dropping his head and swearing under his breath. He trudged towards me at the corner of the bar and said, "I could have sworn I begged you to leave me alone, man. I'm legit."

"Fuck off, Roland. I ask, you tell. You've not forgotten that already have you?"

He shook his head. "Hang about, Pitkin. Ben. Benny, Benny Benjamin. Everyone knows you got sacked. I always thought you were bent, in more ways than one and-"

I grabbed a handful of his hair and dragged him round the corner, pinning him to the wall. "You think it matters? Bent or not, copper or not? I could hang you out to dry any time I wanted. Being out of the force, you know what that means, don't you? No code of conduct to adhere to. I can do what I fucking well want. I could print your picture with a big *grass* underneath and pin it in every shop window in town. And neither you nor anybody could do a damn thing about it," I gave him a grin, "and they'd have your bollocks on skewers. You'd best remember that."

"Whoa, Lay off, Mr Pitkin. I'm paid a real graft now, I'm trying to make a proper honest go of it."

I squashed his face into the wall. "You? Honest? Get a grip, we know each other better than that."

"It's true, I swear, I've a babbie due for dropping soon, please, just leave me alone, man."

His shoulders slumped and he looked like he was going to start crying.

I let him go and willed myself to calm down. "Are you going to hear me out or what?"

He scampered back behind the bar, screwed up his face, spat in the rag and rubbed the rim of a wine glass. "I've nothing to say any more. Why don't *you* listen for a change. I'm sober as a judge and deaf as a post. I don't hear, I don't want to hear and it's working out for me just fine, Mr Pitkin."

I held up my hands, showing my palms.

"Look, I'm sorry, Roland. If it's worth anything, I'm truly sorry for anything I did to you that wasn't fair.

I'll leave you alone from now on, I swear down, I just need you to tell me whatever you can about The Joey. I guarantee you'll never see me again." I pulled out a wad of notes and laid them on the bar.

His gaze lingered on the money. "Are you being serious? About leaving me alone, like?"

I nodded. "Just tell me what you can, take the money and see my back for the last time, Roland."

He rubbed his forehead with the rag and closed his eyes. "If you don't know, you don't know and that's fine."

He looked around and leaned in, his fingers shuffling the twenties. "Well I don't know much, but I do know he's got a major temper on him and he's a big fucker with tattoo-"

I banged my balled fist on the bar, shaking the glasses and he flinched, jumping back a few feet.

"Don't you fucking bullshit me," I shouted.

He bumped into a chubby bloke with dyed blonde hair coming out of the club's back office in a pink silk shirt with a beaming smile. He looked at the cowering Fenk, to me, then back at Fenk, who was straightening up and said, "What's up fellas? Got a problem, Roland?"

He forced a smile. "No, no sir."

"Well aren't you going to introduce me to the hunk? Is he single?"

Roland shrugged, getting a kick out of the look on my face. Pink shirt turned to me, "Are you single, doll?"

"Sorry, I'm otherwise engaged."

"You a friend of my dear boy Roland, then?"

Roland started to sweat.

"Kind of. I'm his drugs counsellor, aren't I Roly? Shit, we've been through tough times me and him. All that stealing and whatnot. He's doing very well though. Very well indeed, especially with the temptation of a bursting till under his fingertips. For a compulsive thief and liar-"

Roland gave a nervous smile to Blondie, who's fake tan wore thinner by the second. He jumped in, "Oh no, no, he's making it out way worse than it was, boss. I've not seen him in ages, he's not here to check up on me. He's asking about our old mate Joey, ain't that right, Mr Pitkin?" He looked at me pleadingly.

I ignored him and raised an eyebrow to Blondie. "You can never be too careful though, eh? Addictions can be lifelong struggle-"

"Never mind that talk, we were on about our Joey, just bantering about old times boss. You get on with what you're doing. Don't let us slack-jawing keep you, boss."

Blondie shrugged his shoulders and took a small vial from his pocket. "We've all got naughtiness in our closets. Roland's past doesn't bother me, especially since he knows if he fucks me over, I'll fuck him…over. For good." He uncapped the lid and tapped coke onto his thumbnail.

Roland salivated as Blondie offered me his outstretched digit.

"No thanks, wouldn't be wise in my line of work."

Roland twisted the rag in his hands and said, "Hang on, he's come here asking about Joey.

How is it we've got onto the subjects of my past and my potential murder? Fuck me for good? Fuck me for good? You want to lay off the sniff, boss," turning to look at me for support.

Blondie snorted and laughed. "Joey, eh? Tie mi kangaroo down, sport, tie mi kangaroo down, fuck a wallaby," he sang through an affected Australian accent and giggled to himself.

Roland looked back at me and raised an eyebrow.

I clenched my fists and grabbed the collar of the crooner. Yanked him up on his tiptoes, face to face over the bar. "I've been polite, I've tried to reason. My patience is wearing very fucking thin.

What do you know about The Joey?"

He cackled and whispered, "I like your aftershave."

"I'm not wearing any."

"I know." He flicked his tongue towards my ear so I pushed my knuckle into his temple. He winced and spurted out, "Ouch, take it easy, big boy, I'm delicate." I pressed harder, "A Joey? I don't know any Joey. It's a baby kangaroo is all I can think of. What else can it be? That hurts, you bastard."

Roland pawed at my arm. "Get off him, Pitkin, for fuck's sake. We don't know, I think that's obvious at this point, don't you? Unless you want us to make something up? Let go, man. Just fuck off and get out."

A wave of vertigo swept over me and I only just registered Fenk's words. I felt disoriented and the room spun.

Lack of sleep.
Lack of food.
Lack of everything and anything. *No peace.*

A crowd of people bustled into the bar, cramping the space. Trickles of sweat broke down my back.

I let go and watched pink shirt rub his temple, forcing blood to flow back into the indent and begin to bruise purple. I dizzied, laughter and shouting flicked my nerves.

Roland stared at me and said, "You need a fucking holiday or summot man, before you go too far. Here, one for the road." He took a glass and turned to a whiskey optic.

I focused on the liquid running into it, breathing hard to steady myself. I longed for the burn and the numbness, however temporary. I reached towards the drink. My hand shook. Craving rattled through my body. I picked it up and my reflection twisted in its surface, warping my face; melting into flickering light reflections from the glitterball, forming pairs of eyes streaming tears. I dropped the glass on the bar. Slid it back to Fenk.

The bar filled. Nudges and jostles and shouts of orders breathed down my neck and I needed air. I pushed the notes across and shouted, "Keep the money. But don't give that fucker any, he'll spend it on drugs and rent boys," I said, pointing to Fenk.

Blondie gave him a puzzled look, licking his lips. I left him squirming in his scuffed shoes.

"Rent boys? He's talking shit. Drugs, yes. Rent boys, no."

***

I forced my way through the mob of leather and linen, the reek of sweat and perfume and booze funnelled nausea into my gut. I stumbled into the street between the human cattle and felt a hand dig into my shoulder and fingers pressing into the gun at the base of my spine. A voice whispered in my ear, "Keep walking and do not turn around. If you try and bolt, I'll pull that piece out and do you with it."

I let him push me down King Street, sapped of strength, disengaged. My legs buckled and I fell to my knees in the road. Some young lads pointed, laughing and shouting "lightweight cunt!" A pair of couples walked around me, crossing over the road.

The man dragged me to my feet and down a side alley next to an Irish-themed bar.

He walked me around the back of an overflowing steel bin and pushed my face into the wall, the cool sting of the concrete jolting me.

Wrapped his hand around my neck and dug his fingers into my ribs.

I could feel the breath on my face as he leaned in and said, "I gather you've take an interest in The Joey? It's about time too. You and your fucking police friends are a way off the ball, pal, aren't you? It's not rocket science. The Joey? Call yourself a detective? Now, how would he get the nickname of the Joey? Think about it."

"A friend of Tommy's are you, or just a concerned citizen?" I spat.

He thumped my head into the wall. He let out a giggle and said, "That sick bastard is no friend of mine no more. Nor is The Joey. They're crossing the line big time. You need to stop it. Now get your brain in gear and think. You haven't got long. Thought you'd have worked it out for yourself by now."

"I can't fucking think. I don't know, my head's battered. Stop talking bollocks and get to the point."

"Coppers, eh? Always need us to do your jobs for you. That fat cunt in the bar was right and you didn't even pick it up. Fucking useless, I hope you're handier with that piece. The Joey is the son of a very prominent businessman of this town. Said businessman wants to keep his hands clean and still control the titillation and sex market. So he opens up a members only club and installs his lad in charge.

His lad is not reet in't head, he's a perv. A straight jump's not enough and he's pushing it way too far.

The businessman can't risk doing his own son though, can't afford to have his legit stuff linked to his sick fucking offspring. He's disgusted after finding out what's going down tonight and he wants it stopping. Clean. I can't do anything, nobody from our side will go against The Joey on this, there's too much money in it for them. Major money. And we've been led to believe our members list has a couple of your lot on it, making it hands off, lawwise.

Now, you can stop it and get the girl out of there. Do you know where there is yet?"

I thought back to pink shirt, what he sang, and my mind sharpened. I knew the place by name and gossip in the station. I was too busy working to ever listen to the stories about the boys sneaking off behind their wives backs for a cheap thrill.

"How did you know I was looking for a girl?"

"Tommy told me. That little bastard. He came to me first, but I told him my hands are tied and to get someone else. And here you are. He said you might need some help because you're a fuck up.

This is all I can do for you. And believe me it's for the girl, not Tommy. Certainly not Tommy, the cunt."

"How long have you been following me?"

"Just long enough to make sure you didn't cut yourself shaving," he giggled again. "So I take it you're waking up?"

"Yes. I know where I'm going."

"Good. Don't turn around. Count to ten, then shift it. Make sure the safety is off."

I counted to two and spun round but the owner of the voice had already disappeared into the warren of backstreets at the top of the alley. I heard a faint beep followed by tires screeching into the night.

***

I forced myself to run to the taxi rank, wishing I'd asked the voice how Tommy knew I took calls at the train station. I also wished I'd asked Tommy, but I knew now I'd have just been spoon-fed more bullshit.

A forearm displaying smudged tattoos tapped along to a radio song. A thin face nodded at me through the open window. "Jump in, fella. You look a bit wishy washy. I'm giving you fair warning, old son; you be sick and you're paying the cleaning bill. And that's before I throw you out on your arse."

I climbed into the back of the cab, feeling like I'd boarded a boat on rocky waves. "Open the fucking windows."

"It is open."

"All of them. Now."

"Take it easy. Job's a good un. So where we off then mate?"

"Kangaroo Klub."

"Who's a naughty boy, then?" The driver smirked and winked at me in the rear view mirror.

I reached under my coat and moved the pistol to rest on my thigh, gripped tightly. I returned the wink. "You don't know the fucking half of it. I'm just picking up a friend. Now shut up and drive."

"You're the boss."

I caught my breath and looked at my reflection in the window. It was skewed by drizzle rivulets and faded in the darkness that enveloped us as we left the bright lights of the town centre.

7

The Kangaroo Klub was a gentleman's club with a rumoured reputation of discretion and a range of services that made Amsterdam look amateur. It had never featured on the vice squad's radar and they'd left it alone despite the odd complaint for reasons unknown to myself at the time. I was murder squad and never had any dealings there. Not as a detective, a beat bobby or for pleasure. The voice said it was owned by a bigshot money man and it was all I needed to know to make sense it wasn't touched.

I said to the cabbie, "It's my first time there tonight. Is it any good?"

He laughed wide mouthed under a bushy moustache and I saw the silver fillings on his back teeth in the mirror. "Couldn't tell you myself, mate. I'm happily married. Well, married any rate. My wife would sniff another woman's perfume a mile off, so it's a strict no-no for me. I've heard so though, and I've never drove anybody home from there without a smile on his face. Wonder why they called it the *Kangaroo Klub?* It's because you can jump anything with a pouch, old son." He chuckled again as we ripped through a country lane parallel to the motorway. He veered off down a dirt track and I couldn't miss the establishment.

It was a converted, detached red brick with three floors and a white stone laden driveway. The garden housed a circular grey concrete fountain with a cherub in the centre cascading water as though pissing through a shining pipe. Tall conifer trees stood either side of the grand mahogany front door, swaying in the growing wind. A yellow neon tube outlining a kangaroo flickered, kicking out one leg after the other can-can style. I told the driver to circle and park round the back.

"Leave the meter running. I won't be too long."

"You sure? You can always just give control a bell when you've had your jollies and someone will come and fetch you. It'll save you a fortune."

"I'm picking up a friend, I've told you. I won't be too long." He looked anxious and I didn't want him getting feet cold enough to hit the accelerator so I pulled out a couple of hundred.

"Keep hold of this. Call it a deposit. You get me to where I need to go and whatever's left you can call a tip."

He struggled to keep his eyeballs in his sockets as I got out. I slapped the bonnet on my way to the Klub and gave him the thumbs up, but he was too busy drooling over the money to look up. I let my overcoat sleeve do a good job of covering the pistol.

8

I passed under an ornate archway with thorned rose stems chiselled into the wood. A CCTV camera loomed above my head, fixed on the doorway. A stocky doorman wearing a black bomber jacket over a white shirt and black dickie bow gave me stone face appraisal underneath a mop of slicked curls. Thick scouse accent drawled, "Evening, sir."

I looked over his shoulder and clocked two shaven headed goons playing human gargoyles at the end of the slim hall.

"Please show your membership card to our reception. Have a great evening."

I reached into my inside pocket and left my hand there, moving forward. He lingered for a second, then stepped aside. I wrenched a smile. I couldn't tell if his passive hostility was exclusively for me or part of his general act.

Down the hall, on my right, a bored looking geek in a yellow dickie bow recited, "Welcome to the Kangaroo Klub. Please allow me to sign you in. If you'd like to pass me your members' card, sir, I'll have you through in no time."

"I'm a guest."

He rolled his eyes. "I'm sorry sir, guests must be on the guest list. Tonight, being a very special night, the guest list is blank"

"What's so special about tonight?"

"If you were a member, you'd know."

I whipped out my warrant card and laid it flat on the yellow plastic booth lip, turning my body and leaning in to shield it from the bouncer. "I'm a guest of honour."

He laughed and said, "Well, why didn't you say so in the beginning? You're already a member. I take it this is your first time here. New to the area are you? Just ask Del or Billy to show you the ropes. Have a splendid evening, detective."

"Thank you." I strode up the blue carpeted hallway to more black bomber jacketed backs and the shaven skulls of Del and Billy. They blocked the door, watching the stage and giggling to each other. I cleared my throat and they swirled round.

"Evening boys." I gave them my only smile and flashed the warrant card briefly. Panic kicked in. Two identical faces peered back at me. I considered the possibility I'd started to see double with the insomnia and sweat broke on my forehead, terrified I was entering a waking dream state. I looked harder. Identical features and structure were differentiated by Del on the left having a thin scar running across his cheek. I made a show of reading their security badges sewn into a plastic holder on their sleeves.

The bad shaver had the hottest temper and didn't try to conceal the scowl. His brother whispered 'inspector' in his ear and his eyebrows raised, stretching the stitched skin on his face. He returned the smile and pushed open the yellow door.

I nodded and stepped inside onto a balcony with a mahogany rail and a short staircase to my right. The muffled thuds of a generic dance beat boomed, ringing my ears. A scattering of suited gentlemen sat sipping drinks around teak tables laid out across the open floor. The only lighting came from a strip of blue spotlights that ran across the ceiling pointing in the same direction the men's heads were facing; at the stage. Three silicone strippers pranced around poles to the music in nothing but heels. To the left of the stage, the bar lit up bright white and the group of coppers made the only racket among the patrons. They settled into four tables near the front of the stage. The suit with the skewed tie stood on his chair wolf whistling, but the girls wouldn't make eye contact. Don Iverson sat at the back of the scrum, pulling on his 'tache and necking his drink. I felt the gun and wished I had more than the thirteen bullets it held. My heart started thumping and I jumped at the tap on my shoulder and spun round.

Del stepped back and smirked, "Sorry mate. Didn't mean to startle you. Forgot, you can't come in with your jacket. You need to pass it through the hatch to Danny. He'll give you a ticket."

I tried to slow my breathing. I nodded. Said, "No problem. Can I just go for a piss first? I'm busting."

He looked to Billy, who shrugged. "No worries. I need one myself. I'll come with you. Follow me."

My chest thumped harder as he led us down the stairs, then double backed into the gents' underneath the balcony. The toilet door swung closed behind us, hushing the music. He whistled and stared at the ceiling as we stood at the trough, then asked, "You got a bid on, then?"

"The counter boy, Danny is it? He mentioned it being a special occasion?"

"Yea, it's the auction. It ends tonight. If you like 'em young, you'd best get your bid in. Big, big money coming in from all over mate, I mean ridiculous amounts. But I suppose it's the only way you're going to find a virgin in this town," he giggled. The same giggle triggered a flash of recognition; from the alley. I stared hard at him, and thought back a minute. No let on. It must have been his brother. He walked over to the condom machine, took out a handful of change and said, "Course I'm going to have to do with one of the strippers as usual. They're a lot cheaper, but take my advice, if you want to go upstairs with one at the end of the night, use three of these fuckers per ride. They're riddled pal, I'm telling you. Got a gobble without one once and I pissed lava for a month. If I had the dough I'd love a pop at the young one, though. Oh aye, I'd giv-"

Revulsion reached for the pistol and I interrupted his speech with a bullet to the back of the head, sending it forward into the wall machine as coins descended like a brass and silver waterfall.

Pink and red spatter glowed from the white tiles. I took off my overcoat and wrapped it around the gun. I walked with my head down, quickly back up the stairs and onto the balcony, booming beats melodied with the ringing from the gunshots. Billy stood with his arms folded, eyeing the staggering suit with disdain. I smiled and gestured with the coat. He nodded, then leaned in, shouting into my ear over the music, "You know that knobhead over there? He's one of your lot, in't he? He'd best start behaving."

"Must be new the new DCI. From another area, has to be. I don't know him."

"Me neither. I know Don Iverson and a couple of the others. He used to knock about with my brother years back."

"Forget him, what about the King Street thing? I think we've met, haven't we?"

He shook his head.

"Tommy Rellis is a pal of yours. I'm working for him. You saw me shaving, remember?"

He looked genuinely puzzled and gave me a funny look, starting to worry I was mentally unstable. He looked over my shoulder. "Where's our kid, squeezing out a turd is he?" He giggled the same distinctive giggle, nervousness sweeping into it.

If the voice in the alley wasn't a creation of my own mind, he was aiding and abetting this sickness and I felt justification and the seeds of rage sowing into my being.

"Probably Your bowels empty themselves when you're dead." I grinned and squeezed the trigger, giving him two in the chest and one in the stomach. I pushed him down, speeding up the slump and went back into the blue corridor. Looked at the entrance;

the scouse bouncer was gone. Back to the receptionist. "Danny isn't it? I forgot something."

"Oh yes, my fault, officer. Sling your coat here, I'll get you a ticket."

"No, no, Danny. I forgot," I pushed the gun barrel underneath the hatch pointing it at his gut, "I forgot. As I'm the guest of honour, I want my backstage pass. Do me a favour and open this latch up to the top."

His eyes widened and panic stung his voice.

"It, it doesn't open."

"Bullshit son. It's on runners. It has to in case of a fire. Health and safety. God bless the fussy fuckers, eh?" I showed him my teeth.

"Don't kill me, please, I only work on the till," he begged.

"Fair deal. Open the hatch and I won't kill you."

He stood frozen for a moment then got to work on a plastic crank. The booth hatch lifted and I scrambled over into the office. I put my coat back on and swung the gun towards Danny, huddled against the back wall, shaking.

I walked straight up to him and he started to whimper, "You promised. You promised you'd let me live."

I nodded, let my gun arm fall and said, "I did. I always follow up on a promise. Besides, you're not worth a bullet." I swung my arm back up, catching him just under the ear with a sharp crack of the stock. His eyes rolled and he collapsed to the deck. I shoved him under the window with my foot and gave him a couple more boots. He'd live, but in what state I couldn't give a fuck. I opened the till and stuffed wedges of cash in every pocket and headed out through a panel wood door at the back of the office with my pistol leading the way like a divining rod dredging for the depraved.

9

I ran down the narrow, dingy corridor and turned up a short staircase onto a long landing with three doors on my right.

The first door was wide open. Through a dense fog of cigarette and weed smoke I saw a couple of strippers parading in front of a wall length mirror doing buttock toning exercises. White powder dusted the dressing table in smudging piles.

I cracked open the second door slowly. The room was lit with soft pink lamps on tables either side of a giant bed covered with a plush burgundy quilt. The headboard had cuffs attached at either end, hanging limply. Behind it there was another wall length mirror from the ceiling to the floor. A single red rose lay with its bud on one of the white pillows. Bile rose in my stomach as I moved to the last door. I grabbed the handle and stiffened when I felt a hand on my shoulder.

A scouse voice said, "Whoa, whoa, whoa there, fella. No admittance backstage. Be a good punter and fuck off back where you came from." His sweaty grip tightened and I felt his pulse in his wrist, blending with the muffled music thumping against the wall.

I raised my empty hand with my fingers splayed. "Sorry, guv. Got lost en route to the pisser."

"Well get your way found sharpish or I'll throw you out the bac-"

I ducked and spun under his outstretched arm, pressed the Browning to the base of his spine and sent his intestines to the bare floorboards with two clicks. He dropped to his knees and lolled forward.

Turning back to the door, I kicked it open and struggled to make sense of what I saw. Tabitha lay on a small cot in the far corner, writhing in restless sleep and dressed in a long yellow silk chemise. Beside her, a flame haired woman mopped her brow and whispered to the girl. On a dressing table, two syringes lay on a red bar towel, one empty. A tablespoon and discarded tin foil sheets barely concealed a burnt, congealed residue. The walls were bare and the room was lit by a dangling shadeless bulb.

She paid no attention to my entering so I made myself known by digging the gun into her scalp and said, "You're Tommy's nurse from A and E, aren't you? You fucked up the first time and gave her too much. She needed just enough to keep her quiet, but she's a tough little scrapper judging by the scratches on your arms. Tommy went apeshit and called off the deal and got scared. He found that slither of decency from his rotting soul and finally woke up to what the fuck he was putting his own offspring through. The Joey won't back down on the set up, though will he? Talk. *Talk! Now!* I swear I'll fucking do you anyway, so get yapping." My voice rose to a shout, seeming further away with every word. I slapped her hard across the ear, knocking her off the chair.

She looked up at me. Mascara had smudged under her dilated pupils. She smirked and said, "Tommy knew the deal from the beginning. He knew full well what he was getting into. He only wanted out when he was told his cut of the auction money wasn't as big as he thought it'd be. You're fucked, you know that, don't you? We're protected, you cunt. So fuck him and *fuck you.*" She spat hard on the floor and rubbed at her head.

I tucked the gun into my belt and grabbed her by the hair. Her finger nails dug into the back of my hand, but I was beyond feeling pain. She screamed, so I hit her hard on the back of the neck and she stopped struggling. I dragged her over to the dressing table and snatched the syringe. I jabbed the needle hard into her carotid artery and depressed the plunger. I watched Tabitha as she wept in her sleep.

I picked up the chair and went back to the red room and barged open the door. I fired four rounds into the centre of the mirror and climbed onto the bed. I swung the chair into the mirror, shattering it into thousands of shards.

A man sat in a leather swivel chair with earphones atop his head with his eyes open, frozen in posture. He wore a yellow towelling bath robe, open, revealing scrawny naked flesh beneath. His shock wore off and he lunged for me, ripping out the headphones from the stereo. Bobby Darin crooned "*Dream Lover*' at top note. He drove his shoulder into my waist. Clawed fingers dug into my ribs, nipping at the skin. His teeth gnawed at my stomach through my suit. I drove the butt of the gun into his skull over and over and rolled on top. I stood up, looking down on him. Blood drenched his face. Wild grey eyes flickered and snarled lips pinned back over his filed canines in a vicious grin.

He reached down and stroked his flaccid member.

I pointed the Browning at him. "You're The Joey, I take it?"

He stared into my eyes and masturbated faster.

"The show's over," I said. I winked and shot him in the groin twice, taking half his hand with it.

He snapped into the foetal position, squealing and bucking, the grin long gone.

I raised the gun but didn't want to end his suffering and I had a feeling I'd need to save the thirteenth bullet. I kicked him hard in the temple and he quietened.

I climbed into his room and turned down the stereo. Four laptops sat on his desk. Two played gangbang porn videos. One was the auction site with bids showing worldwide, the money flying as a digital clock in the corner ticked down the remaining three hours. The fourth displayed Manchester airport arrival times. There was a paper pad with handwritten notes about limousine collection services and another timetable I couldn't make out. I collected the paper and snatched a lighter from next to an overflowing ashtray on his desk. Climbed back into the bedroom.

He was wheezing into the duvet and I crushed his scalp with three heavy blows. I wrapped his limp form in the sheets, piled the duvet on top and ripped open a pillow, sending duck feathers swirling into the air. I stuffed the pillow with paper, shoved it underneath him and set it alight. I watched small wisps of black grey smoke form coils. As soon as I smelt the singe, I ran to get Tabitha.

***

In the corridor, a brunette in an electric green thong wept convulsively over the scouse bouncer's entrails. Heavy green eye shadow smudged and trickles of thick mascara drizzled down her cheeks. She cradled his head and I caught sight of her profile. Emma, the girl from the nursing quarters. I watched her grief enter delirium; shaking her head wildly, heaving out "Terry" like a stuck record. I spat on the floor by the embracing couple and carried on past.

10

I stepped over the prone nurse and knelt next to the girl. Her eyes were open but she wasn't conscious. Whatever visions her dream world was playing for her to make sense of her circumstance did little for comfort. I carried her in my arms out of the room. Flames licked from next door and the fire roared, doing little to cover The Joey's shrieks.

Naked women ran toward then past us and round the corner shouting, "Fire!' They raced down another staircase and I followed them with the girl's head bobbing into my shoulder. I reached the landing and a familiar giggle sent my head spinning.

I'd seen two of these faces distort into death just moments ago and now a third smiled and raised his eyebrows at me from the bottom of the stairs, arm extended, propping open the fire exit as the women ran past us barefooted into the gardens.

"You made the party, big fella. The lads were worried you'd not come through to be honest. Congratulations. Didn't think you were up to it to be brutal. Hope my brothers didn't give you too much jip. I should have warned you really, but time was of the essence and this cloak and daggers stuff is not my thing normally. As long as you didn't do 'em too much harm you'll not see me again. Might teach them a lesson in morality anyway, a bit of a hiding. I tried to persuade 'em to help me get her out myself, but there you go. We all have to live and learn at some point. *Cest La Vie.* Go on, get gone."

I didn't know what to say to the man, so I just nodded.

Suddenly panic spread across his face as he looked back up the stairs.

I followed his line of vision and froze.

Emma stood on the landing, bawling through a contorted face, with a handgun pointing down at me. Racked sobs wavered her aim.

The triplet reacted first and slowly ascended towards her. He lowered his voice and soothed, "Emma, come on, give me the gun, love. Come on, cock, let it go."

She screamed, "He killed them! That fucking bastard's killed them! Terry's dead!" The triplet fell back two steps with the blast of the gunshots.

Plasterboard exploded over my head, popping a white dustcloud. A second later a scorching singe tunnelled through the front of my shoulder, spinning me into the wall.

The triplet shouted, "Jesus Christ, put that fucker down," and lunged for her wrist.

I held onto Tabitha over my good shoulder and willed my other hand to raise the Browning with no response. They wrestled and my legs located themselves with the weeping of the young girl. I heard two more gunshots and the voice of the triplet roar,

"You've fucking shot me! You've fucking shot me, Emma!"

Don Iverson's panting form rounded the corner and he snatched Emma by the throat, dragging her back. She gurgled in the choke hold and swung the gun. He locked her arm, twisting her wrist with a sick snapping. We locked eyes and he looked at me in silence for a second. He threw the woman aside and descended to stem the flow from the third triplet's wounds, looking for all the world a vain exercise. I fought off a riptide of emotion mixing with shock reaction as I ran into the hostile weather.

The women huddled together, shivering and arguing hysterically between themselves about what they should do with make up running down their faces in the downpour. A chubby blonde pointed at us and shouted, "Another O.D? Jesus, you'll kill the poor little bitch."

***

I cradled Tabitha's head and got to the taxi. The driver snored with his chin in his chest. I kicked the door and he woke with a jolt. He smiled at me until he registered the girl over my shoulder and the blood seeping down my shirt. Perplexed fear spread across his face and he fiddled with the keys. I slid her on the bonnet and waved the pistol. He stalled the engine and I opened the door, lying her gently on the back seat. I climbed in and said, "Don't speak.

Just do not say a fucking single word. Get us to the Royal Infirmary."

He looked up at the smoke billowing out of the roof of the Kangaroo Klub and did as he was told. I looked through the rear window, watching the sharp-suited gentlemen pour out into the horizontal rain, surrounding the fountain with mobile phones pressed to their ears and panic in their gestures. The cherub had stopped pissing.

The engine kicked and we screeched down the track. The driver hit the brakes and I was thrown forward into the back of his seat.

"What the fuck are you doing? Drive!" I yelled, reaching for the gun.

"I can't. There's somebody blocking the road."

I looked through the windshield and saw the drunken Champagne Charlie still in the same suit from A and E, flapping his arms and sticking his thumbs out.

"Run him over."

The driver twisted around, "What?"

"Run him over. It'll be good for a laugh if nothing else.."

"Well, if you're putting a gun to my head," he shrugged, "you're the boss."

He released the handbrake and gunned the accelerator. The suit looked up at the sky and waved his hands up prayer-like, beaming and waving. He quickly realised the car wasn't stopping for him and his face dropped. He turned and broke into a sprint, white untucked shirt flapping in the wind. We gained to within ten feet and he dived into a clump of reeds. I watched him roll down an embankment through the back window, his form growing smaller as we sped back to town. The cabbie's raucous laughter rattled through the car. Pain endorphins ripped through my bloodstream at breakneck pace.

For a fleeting moment, I felt like smiling.

11

We hit the town centre and passed King Street, still heaving with all-hour customers oblivious to the chaos. Past the sprawling tower blocks on our right and round towards the hospital and up the hill and into the ambulance bay. Two paramedics wheeled a prone form on a stretcher with an oxygen mask.

    I climbed out of the car and picked up Tabitha. The cabbie looked at me in the rearview and said in a sing song voice, "I know, I know. Stay put or you'll come and do me in. Bust a gap in my arse or whatever they say."

    I winked, "Good lad."

    I carried her across the blacktop over my good shoulder and into the A and E waiting area.

    People in plastic chairs snatched swift glances at us and quickly looked away. Another drunk was being pinned to the floor by the two security men as two of his mates looked on laughing with lager cans in their hands. The paramedics got priority and were rushed to resus, so I passed the empty reception desk and walked right into medical admissions, dripping a trail of luminous red splashes on the white tile flooring.

The senior nurse burst into tears at the sight of the girl. She trembled at the sight of my sopping shirt. Panicked, darting eyes flickered between mine and the girl wriggling and whimpering against me.

"Calm down, please. It's not her blood."

She reached out, opening my jacket and pressing against my stomach where smears of The Joey's claret soaked the cotton. I stiffened at her touch and gripped her wrist and said, "It's not all mine either. I took one just above my collarbone. It missed the bone and it's just a nick in the muscle."

She shook her head and gently took Tabitha from my shoulder and into her arms, laid her on the only unoccupied bed.

I closed the cubicle curtains and said, "Get social services, child protection and whatever else there is. Get security and phone police from all neighbouring counties. Under no circumstances let anyone bluff you into letting her be taken. Tell them she's critical or something. I'll be posting her something here in a few days. Please make sure it ends up with her wherever she goes. Got it?"

The nurse nodded her head and wiped tears off her cheek with the back of her tremulous hand.

"You think she'll be all right?"

She nodded again, busy tapping the top of Tabitha's hands for the cannula. "We'll wean her off the stuff. She'll have some nasty withdrawals and a rough few days. It's after that, after the drugs are out of her, I reckon that's where the real healing will start."

I wiped her eyes with the tip of my thumb and stood back to let other nursing staff flying by with a drip on a wheeled frame get close to the bed.

Vanessa tried to insert the needle but her shaking was beyond control. She passed another staff the syringe and turned back to me. She peeled back the lapel of my suit jacket and ripped the tear in the shirt wider. Blood smeared on her gloves.

Her touch jolted me and I brushed her hands away.

She said, "Your wound needs packing and cleaning. It's not going to stop bleeding on its own and it'll get infected if we don't sort it now. You need to lie down."

I turned my back to her. "Something else to do first, love. Take good care of her."

"Wait. Thank you. Thank you for this. I've been worried sick ever since that day he took her."

"I was just doing my job." I left through the curtains and shouted over my shoulder, "Take good care of her."

I followed my own seeped trail back outside and walked into the rain and watched three ambulances speed out of the building in the direction of the Kangaroo Klub with their sirens blaring. Police helicopters swooped over the town. I climbed in the back of the taxi. The driver hummed along to a jazz instrumental on the radio. "Where to now, boss? I was thinking, you get me a fancy hat and I'll be your chauffer. You've certainly livened up my weekend, old son."

I raised my eyebrows, "One more stop and home. I'd love to give you a job but I prefer to travel on public transport if I can."

"Where we going?"

"To see another friend. Go left out of here then straight on. I'll tell you when to turn."

***

I sunk into the backseat and closed my eyes and thought back to when I'd just made inspector. It was early Christmas Eve when they'd had a call about two carol singers going missing.

Me and my gaffer, DCI Tavistock were interrogating a man named Dempsey who'd beat his psychotic wife to death the same day and kept screaming about fallen angels with terror in his mind on constant loop.

Tavistock was on a case of two missing trick-or-treaters from October and a connection rang bells in my head. Don Iverson pulled me out and I told him to get Tavistock but he said it had to be me because I was senior officer given it was Tavistock's kids that were the singers and I had to lead the search. I begged him to tell me they weren't dressed as angels but he wouldn't speak.

The location was right by the last reported sightings of the trick-or-treaters near Tavistock's inlaws, who'd been minding them as both he and his wife, a nurse on the coronary care unit at the Royal Infirmary, were on duty till midnight.

We got to the Dempsey house and I insisted on confirming our worst fears because Don had a daughter himself. I went down into a small cellar under the porch and saw why Dempsey had killed his wife and the demon she said was inside her.

I kept out of enclosed spaces ever since and thought back to Don, saw him ripping at his 'tache in the Kangaroo Klub at the back of the scrum ogling someone else's daughter or sister or niece or mother while the clock ticked down on the girl. Him and Tommy and the voice setting me loose to stop it with different motives from the same wellspring of cowardice. Iverson; just another one of the boys in Blue, doing his best to fit in and hating himself for it, for the sake of a pension that would be whipped out from under him by the time he'd go to take it like the nurse, Vanessa, from the medical admissions who'd be lucky to have a hospital to work in when the money would be eventually diverted to fuck knows what by a government hell bent on doing away with providing for the vulnerable who couldn't help themselves. Crumbling care facilities and fractured justice next door to plush gentleman's clubs scented with opulence.

Then I thought to Tavistock, who was buried with his children after hanging himself on New Year's Day.

I remembered the red carnations with their blooms bowed over the headstones as they decomposed in the frost at the snow scattered grave.

***

I opened my eyes at the sound of the driver's chirp, "This the gaff, old son?"

"This is it. Park down the alley, cut the lights and keep your head down. I won't be long."

12

Tommy Rellis' place was on the third floor of a sixteen story high rise on the edge of the town centre. I told the cabbie to stay awake this time. The entrance was covered in illegible graffiti and the door flailed on a hinge, baying in the wind. A gust followed me up the pitch dark stairwell, howling. I was relieved to see lights behind the frost glass panel.

I knocked with no response, took two steps back and took it off its hinges. It slapped the floor and rushed a cloud of dust into the air. I crept down the hallway and listened. Nothing. I drew the pistol and charged into the room.

Tommy was stood on step ladders in the centre of the bare room, facing me as I entered. His head was looped into a noose made of thick rope and suspended from an exercise pull-up bar jutting out high up on the ceiling. His hands were pushed together, prayerlike, in front. "I'm glad to see you're embracing spirituality. Have you been praying for forgiveness?"

"I've been waiting for you, Mr Pitkin. You're fee is over there. Take what you've earned." He shifted his eyes to bricks of fifties stacked neatly in the corner.

"I will. Been waiting long? I mean, your legs must be aching, surely? Aching and throbbing and ready to just rest and take the weight off. Don't mind me."

"I did a bad thing, Mr. Pitkin. A very bad thing. This is what I deserve. Don't try and talk me out of it. It won't work."

His face tried hard for sincerity but it looked to me like it had never had enough practise. I stared at the pathetic fucker, rubbed my eyes and pocketed the gun. I sat down on the worn couch and said, "Tommy, some people are sick. Ill, mentally. You understand what I mean? They need treatment, help, reformation. Professional input in a safe environment. Proper food, a bed, sleep and people to listen to their struggles and–."

"Well, I was determined to do this, Mr Pitkin. But you make a lot of sense mate," he smiled.

"You however, are not ill. You're bad. You're just bad, Tommy. No hope for mending you is there?"

"Well, I don't know about that. Bit harsh if you ask me. This is definitely a wake up call."

"I don't want to ask you though, do I? I want to tell you I know the only reason you phoned me was because you wanted all the auction money for yourself. And I tell you what, you're a cracking voice actor. You had me convinced on the phone, you certainly did. Very well done. In person though, it's a bit different, with the non-verbals and suchlike. On top of that, you still haven't asked if she's still alive or even alright, come to think of it."

"I was going to. I was, I swear I was, Mr Pitkin," he stammered.

"I'm sure you were. Maybe changing you isn't just a pipe dream, is it? Maybe there's something in you I can salvage. That sounds like a warm little fantasy to me though, Tommy. Fantasies and daydreams and kidding ourselves from the truth are all well and good, but there's nothing you can do when reality comes storming in and gives you the hard cold shoulder."

I stood up and walked through the kitchen and rummaged through the cupboards. Thousands of pounds were stuffed tightly across the shelves and barely hidden behind the drainage pipes under the sink. More notes had been packed in pans.

I re-entered the living room and walked towards him and watched his fingers scramble desperately at the knot of the noose.

"I asked you for every penny to return her alive. Every fucking penny."

"Pitkin, wait -"

I kicked the stepladders from under him.

Panicked bulging eyes fixed on mine. One hand managed to grip the pull-up bar above his head and he heaved himself up, relieving pressure from his throat. I thumped the butt of the Browning against his knuckles until I heard cracking bones.

I sat down on the couch, Tommy's legs bucking wildly behind my head. I filled piles of large manila envelopes to bursting with all the money and peppered them with stamps. Wrote *Tabitha Rellis, private and confidential, Medical Admissions Unit, Royal Infirmary*. I leaned back into the couch and rested my eyes, weariness hitting deep into my being, dizziness spiralling with blood loss. I waited a wait that seemed like forever until Tommy stopped flailing and all I could hear was the friction creak of a swinging rope. I dragged myself up and let myself out with the envelopes tucked under my good arm, making sure to keep them free of bloodstains.

13

I ignored the cabbie's jovial banter on the way to the train station. I emptied my overcoat pockets of Kangaroo Klub money and handed it all over. I was glad it left him speechless because I had no goodbye for him. I stuck the brown envelopes in the post box and said a silent prayer they'd find her.

I walked into the deserted train station and looked over at the ticket master in the window.

He gazed up from his paperback and hollered, "Maybe tonight's the night, sir," through a wide smile that dissipated when he saw the blood.

"Maybe it is. Maybe it is."

I took the stairs two at a time and strolled across the desolate platform to the bench. The wind whipped furiously under the metal shelter, rattling branches on the other side of the tracks. The rain faded to a drizzle. I sat down, pulled up my collar and huddled my chin into it. I took out the blister pack of Diazepam and popped some yellows, swallowing dry. The phone rang and I let it ring. I daydreamed that I visited the girl at the hospital.

She wouldn't talk to me but the senior nurse Vanessa smiled and said I shouldn't take it personally because she doesn't talk to anyone. I told them both I understood and handed over the envelopes personally, leaving them on her bed, and said that if anyone she was unsure of came to visit she should tell them that Mr P., her social worker, has banned them and they should just go to Hell.

I swung the pistol round and round my finger and remembered the thirteenth bullet and ignored the ringing telephone and ignored the muffled gibberish from the megaphone and ignored the blood draining from me. The surrounding siren wails closing in and helicopter jutting and hovering overhead beaming down light only triggered another daydream of a golden train gliding into the station and sidling to a halt just in front of me and my family and my friends and the girl and my love holding our baby stepping onto the platform to embrace me and walk me on the train and the smiles on the faces of the people on either side with the smell of sweet perfume and warmth from their hands and tickets that said *far far away*. The biting wind blew away the dream and approaching echoing footsteps helped give the dying embers of it the hard cold shoulder. Still, I sat and waited for Hope.

I looked down the tracks flanked by scruffy brambles and thickets and couldn't see any lights, only the blackness of an empty tunnel.

After The Eve

DI Pitkin watched the glass vibrate as Clive Dempsey howled and screeched a wordless shriek of horror. His reddened eyes streamed and slaver dripped in long strings from his open mouth as the screaming rattled through the station. He stared ahead, watching playbacks of memories he wouldn't or couldn't share with others as Pitkin debated which it was.

DCI Tavistock paced into the observation area carrying two Styrofoam coffees with fret etched on his stubbled face. He nodded at Pitkin and handed him a cup. "I thought that two way mirror was soundproofed?"

"It normally is boss. This guy is making one hell of an exception of it."

"So I can hear. What have we got?"

"We've got a live one. Smashed the fuck out of his wife's skull."

"Weapon?"

"No. Bashed her head repeatedly into the corner of their archway in the living room. And I mean bashed. Back of the head caved in, brains everywhere. Neighbours heard a scuffle but what made them call was the screaming. They thought it was her, turns out it was him. He's still doing it as you can hear."

"No let up at all?"

"Not even a pause for breath He wouldn't even let us get someone to tend to the wounds on his arms."

Tavistock leaned closer to the window taking in the open gashes on the forearms and biceps on Dempsey. "Deep marks, sure are some defence wounds. Looks like he's been clawed by a fucking panther. How old was the victim?"

"Fifty eight."

"That's a hell of a fight for a fifty eight year old. Definitely no one else involved?"

Pitkin shook his head and winced as he swallowed the scalding coffee. "No signs of a third person. Back door was double locked from the inside, nothing from the interior suggests more than a raging fight. Neighbours don't identify any other comings and goings in the past few days in the whole street apart from carol singers."

Tavistock nodded, eyeing Dempsey. "Ok. Motive?"

"Well, from the medical records, it appears she went psychotic. This is the second episode. First was around mid-October lasting until mid-November. Talked about a demonic forces. Being possessed. They both took early retirement in September and it started just after that. Seems the husband freaked, or got pissed off with the thought of nursing her when she went through another nutso period. He's the main carer, something made him snap."

"At half six on Christmas Eve?"

"Of all the days, right? That's all we've got to go on so far but it looks open and shut. The why is just guesswork until he starts talking. He ain't saying a dickie bird. How you getting on with the missing kids?"

"I'm not. Done the local sex offenders and all the other dodgy fuckers. Nothing as yet. Seven weeks is a long time for turning nothing up. All the green areas swept, lakes, canal and ponds dredged. Not even a scrap of clothing. It doesn't look good. I'm praying for a ransom note. Vigilantes are out kicking down doors of fucking paediatricians and God knows who else. No leads."

"Have you given up on the possibility of a snatching?"

"No suspect vehicles, no CCTV footage worth a shit. It's possible, but we closed up a ten mile radius hours after the report from the parents. Tore their house to pieces too, just in case, but they definitely have nothing to do with it."

"After I've written this up, I'll help you go through the information again. See if anything got missed."

"Thanks Pitkin. So what about Dempsey? I don't buy he got scared at the thought of looking after her. When people get fed up they'll smother or pull the life support machine plug out. They won't smash their fucking skulls in. Look at the defence wounds on his arms. If they are defence wounds. Some are from a strange angle as if he was being pulled back. Doesn't resemble a mercy killing. He was either fighting for his life or he was freaked. What did the duty doctor say?"

"He said fuck all, as usual. He thinks Dempsey is experiencing some kind of post traumatic shock. You can tell by his eye movements that he is just reliving an image over and over again. He's given him some tranquilizers, but they haven't even touched the sides."

Tavistock nodded, nudged Pitkin and said, "Fuck it, let's go have a word with the screaming banshee."

"After you, boss," he replied with a theatrical bow. The two exited the side door of the observation area and approached the interview room door. Nodding at the uniformed copper, Pitkin asked, "Anything coherent said, Jimmy?" He frowned and shook his head.

"Just screaming and crying. Poor bastard looks like he's scared stiff. He's freaking me out to be honest. God knows what he's seen."

"His wife's brain matter ruining the carpet probably," grinned Tavistock.

Pitkin entered first, clicked on the recorder and was followed in by Tavistock who clicked it back off. He tried to catch Tavistock's eye, but the DCI was fully focused on the twisted features of Clive Dempsey, howling and dry heaving racked sobs.

"Clive? Clive? Oi! Hello? Clive, I know you can hear me Ok, so I suggest you listen and listen good. You're fucked. You understand? No way out of this one. Talk to us and the one thing we can do is get you out quicker. Make sense? Mitigating circumstances. What did she do? Catch her fucking around? Hen peck you, one nag too many? Come on Clive, we've all felt badgered. Talk to me."

Clive Dempsey continued to stare straight ahead with his pupils dilated and his jaw hanging, drool and snot mixed with tears as he wept openly and began to shake his head. Pitkin sat down opposite him, "Come on Dempsey, get talking for your own sake!

Couldn't stand looking after her? No shame in that. Not sure smashing her fucking head in is anything to be proud of though, is it? Help us understand why you killed your wife. Come on man!" He banged his fist on the table which Dempsey did not seem to register as he shook his head faster.

Tavistock hunted for Clive's stare. He waved his hand in front of the hysterical man's unblinking eyes and nodded. He picked up the plastic chair next to Pitkin and threw it down hard next to Dempsey, crashing into the tiled floor. He sat shoulder to shoulder with him, stared at his head inches away and whispered in his ear, "Clive, she was a fucking pain in the arse, wasn't she? Pestering every minute of the day. You dreaded finishing work, didn't you? Spending every hour of the day listening to the nagging old bitch?" Dempsey shook his head faster and rubbed at his balding head as his flexing muscles tensed, re-opening the wounds on his arms. He continued, "Bollocks. Then she starts to go all weird on you, we know Clive. Starts talking about a demon inside her, doesn't she Clive? Seems strange but she comes out of it, a one off. Then it recurs, doesn't it? Mid December? You can't live like that, can you? It all gets on top of you. You're trying to get in the festive mood, celebrate the birthday of Our Lord and all, sorting out the turkey and then she's off with the fairies talking about fallen angels and all that bollocks. It's too much and you snap. Understandable. You tell her to shut up. She keeps screaming and babbling in your face and you lose control and grab hold of her. She stumbles back, cracks her head then lashes out so you instinctively finish the job. You're shocked, stunned and can't believe what you've done. You're sorry and you don't know what came over you. How am I doing Clive?"

Dempsey rattled his head side to side, heaved again and vomited bile over the interview table. He croaked, "It came over her. It wasn't Clara. Oh those fallen angels!" He let out a piercing cry, jolting Tavistock to recoil. He looked over at the shaken Pitkin, mouthed 'Clara', who mouthed back 'wife'. He nodded and loosened his tie.

"I'm sorry Clive. I just want the truth. What came over her? Please, take deep breaths. Slower, that's it. Close your mouth, breathe through your nose. Look at me, focus on my face. Let the pictures in your mind fade away and look at me. Breathe slower, nice and easy. Better. What came over her? Her illness?"

Clive stared into the dark eyes of Tavistock, a look of anguish that the experienced detective had never seen before. He gulped hard and in a tremulous voice said, "They said it was an illness. Psychosis. She knew it wasn't. She knew it was a demon. I didn't believe her, nobody did. And look what happened. Those poor fallen angels!" He roared, and fell back screaming and rocked in the chair. Pitkin waved at his boss, motioned toward the door, got up and was followed out and back into the observation area.

"What do you think, lad?"

Pitkin replied, "Sir, I'm not sure at all, but I'll tell you he's putting shivers up my fucking back, and I don't mind admitting it. Do you believe in all that demon talk?" He asked, blushing and sweeping his blonde fringe from his clean shaven face.

"Nope. Don't believe in angels either. Fallen angels? What's that all about? He sounds as mental as his wife. A folie a deux."

Pitkin frowned, "Sorry?"

"Shared delusions. When lovers start to believe each other's outlandish beliefs. Fallen angels though, that's what's sending him over the edge. If we give him five and then go back in, we can clear this up and have last look at the missing kid's info. If nothing jumps out we can fuck off home before twelve and I can get all the presents under the tree for the morning. My two are at my sister-in-law's until the wife finishes her shift at the hospital. She's going to pick them up and have them in bed before I get home. Otherwise the little buggers will have ripped all their boxes open and left nowt for Christmas Day." Tavistock said and laughed, a rare glow accompanying his tight smile. "What have you got planned kiddo? A night on the tiles?"

"No boss. Quiet one in front of the telly. Couple of beers. I'll be doing the early shift tomorrow. Sorting out all the paperwork on this bastard."

"No bird on the scene?"

"None of them are that serious. I just can't choose, call me picky." He smirked.

"You'll settle down one day. A wife and kids, that's what makes a man of you sunshine." Tavistock patted at his suit jacket pocket, "Left my mobile in my car. Bollocks. Doesn't matter, we'll be done soon. Come on, let's sort out this fallen angels nonsense."

Pitkin led the way back into the interview room. Dempsey was slumped over the table, exhaustion mixed with the pills from the doctor. The screaming had subsided into a low nasal sighing. Tavistock walked over to the killer and again, sat by his side.

"Sit upright please, Clive. Now I want you to listen very carefully. I want you to see those images in your mind for what they are. Images, that's all. Just images. You can't touch them. Now I want you to make the pictures smaller, that's it. Now lessen the colour and send the picture further away in your mind." Tavistock watched as Dempsey followed his instructions and began to calm. "Now Clive, describe to me what you are seeing. Take your time and remember to keep the images a distance back."

Pitkin watched from the corner of the room as Dempsey slowly sat upright and again widened his eyes, then switched on the recorder.

"She is there. But she isn't. It's not her. It has taken over again. She is ripping up pages from the Bible again. Thousands of little pieces, throwing them around the room as she screams for me to get out. It's not her voice. It's not her. I'm scared and I tell her to remember it's me, her husband. She shows her teeth and I back out into the kitchen to find the number of her social worker to get the doctor again. I can't find it and my hands are shaking. I turn up the radio to hear Christmas songs and drink some whiskey out of the bottle to stop the shaking, but it doesn't work. I sit down and turn the radio louder. I rummage in the cupboards for her tablets from the psychiatrist and pop two from the foil into a cup and run a glass of water. I drink more whiskey but my hands won't stop shaking." Dempsey spoke with a flat tone and tears ran down his cheeks.

"It's alright, Clive. Go on. Shrink the image and keep it at a distance. That's it. Carry on," prompted Tavistock, gently.

"I, I, just sat there. Just sat there. If I had have gone sooner. If only I had gone sooner." He sobbed harder.

Tavistock nudged his shoulder and said, "What's done is done, Clive. Keep going, you are doing well. What then, Clive?"

"I opened the kitchen door and she, no it, it, it wasn't her. It had taken them. Taken them down into the floor. Those poor angels. Fallen, fallen angels. I grabbed her, no, no, it. I grabbed it and had to destroy it for what it had done to those poor, poor fallen angels. So I grabbed it and it was so strong. So strong. It wasn't her, it changed her face, her, her teeth were sharp and fingers were curled with sharp bone, her hair was up on ends and there was blood on her dress. I thought it was dead and went after those poor angels, fallen in the floor and saw the others. It ripped at me from behind, at my arms, it was too late, the angels the poor angels had fallen and they couldn't come back and I turned and killed it. I pushed its head into the wall with all my strength over and over. That's all I can see, over and over. Over and over. It won't stop, help me make it stop. Help me, help me. Please, I beg you!" He screamed and his body bucked in panic. Pitkin and Tavistock struggled with an arm each as Dempsey tried to drive his head into the wall, knocking over the table.

A uniformed officer ran in and took the arm from Pitkin, who stood back and saw DC Iverson beckoning him at the door. Iverson locked the interview room after he exited and ran his fingers through his ginger moustache. "We've had a phone call. Two more kids reported missing. Not returned from carol singing since about five-ish this afternoon. Brother and sister, seven and nine."

"Well, why pull me out? Tell the boss, he's dealing with the others from the end of October. Could be related Don."

"It's got to be you. You're the most senior on duty. Apart from the boss. He can't get involved though."

"What you mean, he can't get involved?"

"It's his kids who are reported missing, Pitkin."

"Jesus Christ. Where are we up to?"

"All uniform scouring the locality. Door to door, every house in the surrounding area. Five mile traffic radius set up and closing in, all the traffic boys with their lights on. Christmas fucking Eve. Like Halloween all over again. Fucking hell, Inspector," replied Iverson, nausea ripping through him.

"Halloween?"

"October thirty first. The first two kids, brother and sister. Out trick or treating. Vanished."

Pitkin stared at Iverson and bolted to Tavistock's office. He flipped through bundles of print outs, tossed them aside and looked up at the wall. Two photographs. School portraits, he guessed both between eight and ten. He looked down at the desk and saw a family photo in a frame. Tavistock with his arm around his wife and the two children in front smiling for the camera. His knees buckled as he looked at the far wall with the map pinned up. He double checked the addresses and ran his finger over the black and grey as his hand started to shake.

"Where does the sister-in-law live, Iverson?"

"Twenty five Piermount View."

"Oh no. Fuck me, no," Pitkin spat through a broken voice as he dropped to one knee.

"What? Inspector, what?"

"It's four streets away from the Dempsey's. They were dressed as angels, weren't they? Tell me they weren't, Don, say they weren't," he pleaded.

Iverson dropped his head, "How did you know?"

"Oh Jesus, oh God." Pitkin ran back into the observation area and stared through the two way mirror. Tavistock sat next to Dempsey with a concerned arm draped over the man's shoulder as he listened to him talk. Pitkin then turned and sprinted towards the station car park with Iverson following.

Inside the interview room Dempsey sat, dazed and worn. Tavistock probed again, "Clive, tell us about the floor. What does through the floor mean?" Dempsey stared ahead, blinked hard as his eyes rolled back and his body convulsed. "Clive? Clive? Can you hear me? Get the doc! Now, for fuck's sake!" He yelled at the uniform.

***

Pitkin floored the accelerator, roaring through the December evening, past the lit windows, fairy lights and snowmen in the gardens. "Iverson, what's the address of the first two missing kids?"

"Four Eight Two Bexley Gardens."

"Where's that?"

"Near the Heath. About half a mile from Piermount."

"Fuck." Pitkin ran through the red lights and pushed eighty down the bypass, screeching the roundabout and up to the Heath. He skidded to a standstill and exited the vehicle. Approaching the house, a uniform shouted for him to slow. Pitkin clipped the copper on the jaw and headed into Eleven Heath Road. Red brick modern detached. Iverson went in behind, flashing his identification at the prone and stunned P.C.

Pitkin ripped through the blue and white tape, headed through the porch and into the living room. He flicked on the light and took in the scene. Blood spatters trailed the beige carpet and a metallic stench hung in the air. A blue vase lay in shards and a coffee table was upturned, the floor was covered in bits of paper. Crimson smeared down the oak wood archway. He scanned the room again as Iverson caught up with him.

"Don, give me a hand here," shouted Pitkin as he gripped the edge of the carpet, pulling it free from the tacks. Iverson followed suit and together they rolled it back, revealing bare floorboards. Adrenalin tore through their veins and cold sweat matted their shirt backs. He shook his head and swallowed the vomit that had risen to his throat. Iverson yanked at his moustache as his eyes darted around the room.

Pitkin closed his eyes and replayed the noises of Iverson's arrival. He opened them and swung back towards the porch as the hollow clops rang in his ears. He pulled back a rectangular red patterned Turkish rug that was soaked in melting grey slush and took a long look at the trapdoor. "You have kids, Iverson?"

He nodded, twitching. "One."

"Best give me your torch."

"Pitkin, let me. I've seen bad things before."

Pitkin shook his head. "Somebody has to have a Christmas."

Together they heaved open the trap door. A set of wooden steps disappeared into the darkness. Pitkin flicked the torch on and made the descent as Iverson lit a cigarette and stared at the ceiling, mumbling prayers as the smoke bobbed between his lips.

The screams jolted Iverson and the butt fell from his mouth making a light tap on the flooring.

Slow, heavy footsteps thudded back up the stairs.

Iverson took in the blank stare of Pitkin.

Pitkin looked at Iverson and nodded. "Four fallen angels."

He walked through the house into the kitchen and snatched Clive Dempsey's whiskey, swallowing hard as he followed Iverson out the door. "You mind driving, Don? Only I could use some Christmas spirit," he said as he shook the bottle.

The silence on the drive back was deafening as the unmarked police car cruised through the deserted streets.

They approached the station that rang unusually hollow.

The desk sergeant saw them enter and lowered his head at the sight of Pitkin's face. They made their way down the stairs and along the corridor, squeezing past a throng of uniforms trying in vain to calm a woman in a nurse's uniform and restrain her from entering the observation area. "Give me five minutes and then let her in, boys," shouted Pitkin, as he and Iverson walked towards the two way mirror.

They watched as Tavistock fed Clive Dempsey hot coffee in small sips.

"Pitkin, you want me to tell him?" He watched as Pitkin drained the rest of the whiskey.

"Go home Don, it'll be twelve pretty soon. Like I said, somebody has to have a Christmas."

Printed in Great Britain
by Amazon